Here's what kids have to say to
Mary Pope Osborne, author of
the Magic Tree House series:

*If you didn't make the Magic Tree House Books
I would go nuts!!!!*—Anthony

*Jack gave me the idea of getting a notebook
myself.*—Reid K.

*I hope that you make more Magic Tree House
books. They bring magic to my life.*
—Michell R.

You gave me the courage to read. Thanks!
—Lydia K.

*I like your books because they are very exciting.
It's like I'm traveling around the world with
Jack and Annie.*—Elizabeth C.

Our imaginations are soaring thanks to you!
—Julie M.

Your books inspired me to read, read, read!
—Eliza C.

*Reading your books gave me the idea to write
a book myself.*—Tyler

*I think your books are great. I can't sleep
without reading one.*—Leah Y.

Teachers and librarians love Magic Tree House books, too!

You have created a terrific tool for motivating children to learn about historical moments and places.—L. George

As a teacher I love how easily your books tie in with curriculum studies. Science and Social Studies units can easily be supplemented using your series. . . . Your books let my students experience other places and times beyond their front door.—T. Gaussoin

Due to your wide variety of settings, my students are learning an invaluable amount of information about history and the world around them, sometimes without even realizing it.
—L. Arnts

It amazes me how these books easily lured my students into wanting to read.—T. Lovelady

Dear Readers,

Last year, while my husband Will and I were doing research for our Magic Tree House Research Guide on rain forests, we visited the Bronx Zoo in New York. As we passed by the gorilla area, we saw a large gorilla sitting under a tree. She was staring very intently at us. We said hi to her—and she stuck out her tongue at us! I'm convinced she was just trying to make us laugh. And we did! In fact, we <u>still</u> laugh whenever we think about that moment.

We found out later that the gorilla's name is Pattycake. I keep a photograph of Pattycake on my desk, and I feel as if she's a giant, friendly spirit who overlooks all my work.

I love gorillas more than I can say. And I hope that by the time you finish reading <u>Good Morning, Gorillas</u>, you'll love them as much as I do.

All my best,

Mary Pope Osborne

Good Morning, Gorillas

by Mary Pope Osborne

illustrated by Sal Murdocca

A STEPPING STONE BOOK™

Random House 🏠 New York

For Dr. Michael Pope

Text copyright © 2002 by Mary Pope Osborne
Illustrations copyright © 2002 by Sal Murdocca

www.randomhouse.com/magictreehouse

Library of Congress Cataloging-in-Publication Data
Osborne, Mary Pope.
Good morning, gorillas / by Mary Pope Osborne ; [Sal Murdocca, illustrator].
p. cm. — (Magic tree house ; #26) "A stepping stone book."
SUMMARY: The magic tree house takes Jack and Annie to an African rain forest,
where the siblings encounter gorillas and learn to communicate with them.
ISBN 0-375-80614-8 (trade) — ISBN 0-375-90614-2 (lib. bdg.)
[1. Gorillas—Fiction. 2. Human–animal communication—Fiction.
3. Time travel—Fiction. 4. Magic—Fiction. 5. Tree houses—Fiction.]
I. Murdocca, Sal, ill. II. Title.   PZ7.O81167 Go 2002   [Fic]—dc21   2002017828

Printed in the United States of America   First Edition   July 2002
10 9 8 7 6 5 4

Random House, Inc.   New York, Toronto, London, Sydney, Auckland

Contents

Prologue

One summer day in Frog Creek, Pennsylvania, a mysterious tree house appeared in the woods.

Eight-year-old Jack and his seven-year-old sister, Annie, climbed into the tree house. They found that it was filled with books.

Jack and Annie soon discovered that the tree house was magic. It could take them to the places in the books. All they had to do was point to a picture and wish to go there. While they are gone, no time at all passes in Frog Creek.

Along the way, Jack and Annie discovered that the tree house belongs to Morgan le Fay. Morgan is a magical librarian of Camelot, the long-ago kingdom of King Arthur. She travels through time and space, gathering books.

In Magic Tree House Books #5–8, Jack and Annie help free Morgan from a spell. In Books #9–12, they solve four ancient riddles and become Master Librarians.

In Magic Tree House Books #13–16, Jack and Annie have to save four ancient stories from being lost forever. In Magic Tree House Books #17–20, Jack and Annie free a mysterious little dog from a magic spell. In Magic Tree House Books #21–24, Jack and Annie help save Camelot. In Magic Tree House Books #25–28, Jack and Annie learn about different kinds of magic.

1

Dark and Rainy

Tap-tap-tap.

Jack sat up in bed. Rain tapped against his window. His clock said 5 A.M. It was still dark outside.

Annie peeked into his room.

"Are you awake?" she whispered.

"Yep," said Jack.

"Ready to find some special magic?" she asked.

"Maybe we should wait," said Jack. "It's so dark and rainy."

"*No* waiting," said Annie. "I'll get an umbrella. You bring a flashlight. Meet you downstairs."

"Okay, okay," said Jack.

He jumped out of bed. He pulled on his clothes and put on a jacket. Then he grabbed his backpack and flashlight.

Jack slipped downstairs and out the front door. Annie stood on the porch in jeans and a T-shirt. The air was chilly and breezy.

"Don't you need a sweater or something?" said Jack.

"I'm okay," she said. "Let's go."

Annie raised the umbrella. Jack turned on the flashlight. They followed a circle of rainy light down their street into the woods.

They headed through the Frog Creek woods. The flashlight lit up the trees—the wet leaves and dark branches. Then it shined on a dangling rope ladder.

Jack raised the flashlight beam.

"There it is," he said.

A circle of light lit the magic tree house.

"Morgan's not there," said Annie. "I can tell."

"Maybe she left us a message," said Jack.

Jack grabbed the rope ladder and started up. Annie put the umbrella down and followed. When they climbed inside, Jack shined the flashlight around the tree house.

Morgan le Fay wasn't there. But the scrolls from their trip to old England were.

"Here's proof we found a special magic yesterday," she said.

"Yeah," said Jack, smiling. "*Theater* magic." He had great memories of acting in a play by their friend William Shakespeare.

"Did Morgan leave us a new secret rhyme?" asked Jack.

He shined the flashlight on a a book lying under the window. A piece of paper was sticking out of the book.

"Yes!" said Annie. She picked up the book and pulled out the paper.

Jack shined his light on the paper while Annie read aloud:

Dear Annie and Jack,

Good luck on your second journey to find a special magic. This secret rhyme will guide you:

To find a special kind of magic
in worlds so far apart,
speak a special language,
talk with your hands and heart.

> *Thank you,*
> *Morgan*

"What kind of language does she mean?" Jack asked.

"I guess we'll find out," said Annie. "Where are we going?"

Jack shined the flashlight on the cover of the book. It showed huge trees partly hidden by mist. The title was:

AN AFRICAN RAIN FOREST

"*Rain* forest?" said Jack. "Good thing we brought our umbrella and flashlight. Remember the rain in the *Amazon* rain forest? Remember how dark it was under the treetops?"

"Yeah," said Annie. "Remember the spiders and scary ants?"

"Well . . . ," Jack said, "not all rain forests have the same bugs."

"Remember the river snakes?" said Annie. "And the crocodiles?"

"Well . . . ," said Jack, "not all rain forests have big rivers. There are different kinds of rain forests, you know."

"Right," said Annie. She pointed to the cover of the book. "I wish we could go there."

The wind started to blow.

"Oh, remember the jaguar?" said Annie. "And the vampire bats?"

"Wait!" said Jack.

But it was too late. The wind was blowing harder. The tree house started to spin.

It spun faster and faster.

Then everything was still.

Absolutely still.

2

Cloud Forest

Jack opened his eyes.

"I can't tell *what* kind of rain forest this is," said Annie. She stared out the window.

Jack looked out, too. It seemed to be daytime, but he couldn't see much of anything. The quiet forest was covered with fog.

Jack opened their research book and read:

> **The misty rain forest in the mountains of central Africa is called a "cloud forest."**

"Oh, I get it," said Annie. "We're up so high, it's like we're in a cloud."

"Cool," said Jack. He pulled out his notebook and wrote:

cloud forest—rain forest high

up in mountains

Then he read more:

**The African cloud forest is home to
many animals, including elephants,
water buffaloes, black leopards . . .**

Jack looked up.
"Black leopards?" he said.

"Don't worry," said Annie.

Jack cleared his throat and kept reading:

. . . antelopes, wild hogs, and gorillas.

"*Gorillas?*" said Annie.

"Don't worry," said Jack.

"I'm not worried. I *love* gorillas," said Annie. "They're totally great!"

"I don't know about that," said Jack. He pictured huge apes pounding their chests. "I'd like to study them, though. Write down their habits and behavior, just like a real scientist."

"Whatever," said Annie. "Let's just go. This'll be a fun adventure!" She took off down the ladder.

Jack threw his notebook, the research book, and the flashlight into his pack. He hooked the umbrella over his arm. Then he followed Annie.

When they stepped onto the ground, Jack could see better. The fog had turned into a fine mist.

Jack and Annie started through the cloud forest. They walked around huge trees draped with moss. They pushed past tall shrubs and leafy plants.

"Wow, look at *that* tree," said Annie.

She pointed to a fat tree. It had wide lower limbs padded with thick cushions of moss.

"It looks like a piece of furniture," said Annie, "like an armchair."

"Yeah," said Jack. "I better draw it."

He put the umbrella on the ground. He pulled the flashlight out of his pack and put it next to the umbrella. Then he took out his notebook and pencil.

As Annie walked ahead, Jack started to draw a simple picture of the fat tree.

"Hey, Jack," Annie called in a whispery voice. "Come here. Quick!"

Jack grabbed his pack. He moved around the tree and caught up with Annie.

"Listen," she said.

Jack heard branches snap.

Crack!

A leopard? he wondered.

Crack! Crack!

Jack nervously looked around the forest.

"Maybe we should go back up to the tree house," he said. "We could read a little more and learn a little more."

Annie didn't answer. Jack turned to her.

She was grinning from ear to ear as she stared into the bushes. Jack followed her gaze.

A dark, shaggy little head was peeking out from a cluster of leaves.

"*Bu, bu?*" a small gorilla asked.

3

Bu-bu

The gorilla's fur was very black against the green leaves. She had large nostrils and small ears. Her bright brown eyes were full of mischief.

"*Bu, bu, bu,*" she said. "*Bu, bu.*"

"*Bu, bu* yourself," said Annie.

The gorilla hid behind the leaves again. Then she poked her head out.

"Peekaboo!" said Annie.

The gorilla clapped her hands together.

She stuck out her tongue.

Jack and Annie both laughed.

"Bu, bu, bu!" the gorilla said. Then she bounded away through the misty forest.

"Hey, Bu-bu! Don't leave us!" Annie called.

Jack rolled his eyes. "Don't name her Bu-bu," he said to Annie. "You don't have to—"

"Wait, Bu-bu!" Annie shouted. She took off after the small gorilla.

"—turn every animal into your best friend," Jack finished. He shook his head. Then he made a list in his notebook.

gorilla behavior

plays peekaboo

claps hands

sticks out tongue

18

As he wrote, Jack heard Annie laughing. But then he heard high shrieks.

He caught his breath. *A leopard?* he wondered.

Carrying his notebook, Jack hurried in the direction of the noise. He found Annie and the small gorilla perched in two trees.

"What's wrong?" said Jack, standing beneath the trees.

"Nothing!" called Annie. "We're just playing."

The small gorilla screeched again. Then she scratched her head and hiccuped.

Annie screeched, too. She scratched *her* head and hiccuped.

While they played, Jack studied the gorilla a bit more.

He noticed she was about the size of a

three-year-old kid. Her fingers looked like human fingers. They even had fingernails! He made a new list:

<u>young gorilla</u>

size of 3-year-old

fingers like humans'

fingernails

Jack heard the tree leaves shaking. He looked up. Annie and the gorilla had both climbed higher.

"Hey, come down, Annie!" Jack called. "You might fall. Plus, it's getting dark."

Jack looked around. Light was fading quickly from the forest. *Is night falling?* he wondered. *Or is a storm coming?*

The small gorilla screeched again and climbed even higher.

"Hey, Bu-bu! Where you going?" said Annie. She climbed even higher, too.

"That's enough, Annie. Come down *now*!" said Jack. "I'm serious."

To his relief, the gorilla settled on a branch. Annie did the same.

The gorilla broke off a piece of tree bark. She nibbled it like a candy bar.

Annie broke off a piece of bark. She nibbled it like a candy bar, too.

The gorilla threw down her bark. She grabbed a tree branch and swung to another tree.

"Don't try it, Annie!" shouted Jack.

But his warning came too late.

Annie threw down her bark. She grabbed a tree branch and *tried* to swing to another tree.

Annie didn't swing like a gorilla. She fell

from the tree—and crashed down to the
ground near Jack.

"Annie!" he cried.

4

Nightmare

Jack knelt beside Annie. She was gasping for breath.

The gorilla bounded down the tree and over to Annie. She bit her lower lip as if she were worried.

"Are you okay?" Jack asked Annie.

"Yes—" Annie panted, "just—got the breath—knocked out of me—"

"Wiggle your arms and your legs," said Jack.

Annie wiggled her arms and her legs.

"Good, nothing's broken," said Jack.

Just then, he felt a drop of water hit his arm. The mist had turned to rain.

"Uh-oh," said Jack. He threw his notebook into his pack.

"I better get our umbrella and flashlight," he said. "I left them near that tree that looked like a chair."

"I'll come, too," said Annie. She started to sit up.

"No, no, catch your breath," said Jack. "It's not far. I'll be right back."

He took off his jacket and draped it over her. "This'll help you stay dry," he said. He pulled on his pack and stood up.

The gorilla screeched.

"Stay with Annie!" said Jack.

Then he dashed back through the cloud forest. He looked for the fat tree with the wide limbs padded with moss.

As he peered through the growing darkness, Jack saw *many* fat trees. He saw *many* limbs padded with moss.

Soon he could hardly see trees at all. He realized that both a storm *and* night had come to the forest.

Forget the umbrella and flashlight, he thought. It was more important to get back to Annie before it was too dark. They could wait together for daylight.

As Jack started back to Annie, he could hardly see. He didn't know which way to go.

"Annie! Bu-bu!" he shouted. He felt silly shouting, "Bu-bu." But he didn't know what else to call the small gorilla.

Jack put out his hands. He moved slowly through the dark, rainy forest. He kept calling for Annie and Bu-bu. He listened for them. But he couldn't hear anything above the loud patter of the rain.

"Ahh!" he shouted. He had run into something that felt like a ball of spiderwebs!

As he jumped back, he slipped and fell in the mud. He crawled over to a tree and huddled between two of its giant roots.

I'll just wait here until morning, he thought. *Then I'll find Annie. Or she'll find me.*

As rain dripped all around him, Jack wondered if leopards came out at night. He quickly pushed the thought away. He tried to think about morning and finding Annie and going home.

He was *really* ready to go home.

Why did Morgan even send us to the cloud forest? he wondered. He tried to remember the secret rhyme.

"To find a special magic . . . ," he whispered. He couldn't remember the rest. He felt tired and miserable. He took his backpack off and rested his head on it. He closed his eyes.

"To find a special magic . . . ," he mumbled.

But he couldn't find the magic. He couldn't even find the words that finished the rhyme. Worst of all, he couldn't find Annie.

Their fun adventure in the cloud forest had turned into a nightmare.

5

Silverback

Jack felt something tugging on his sleeve. He opened his eyes.

Bu-bu. The small gorilla was staring at him in the dawn light.

Jack stood up. His arms and legs felt stiff and achy. His wet clothes stuck to his skin.

He looked around the cloud forest. Misty sunlight shined through the tree branches.

"Where's Annie?" he asked the small gorilla.

Bu-bu waved her arms. Then she bounded off between the trees. Jack pulled on his pack and followed.

As the small gorilla led him through the cloud forest, her head bobbed above the leafy plants. Finally, she stopped before a row of shrubs.

Jack took a few steps forward and peered over the shrubs.

"Oh, man," he whispered.

Large dark figures were sleeping in an open, grassy area—*gorillas!* There were at least ten of them. Some slept on their backs. Some slept on their bellies.

The gorillas were all sizes. The smallest was a baby sleeping in its mother's arms. The biggest was a giant with black and silver fur.

Jack pulled the book out of his pack. He

found a chapter on gorillas and read:

Mountain gorillas live together in families. The leader of the family is a large male called a "silverback" because he has silver fur on his back and shoulders. Gorillas do not hunt other animals. They mainly eat the plant growth of the forest. They are known to be shy and gentle giants.

"Shy and gentle giants," Jack repeated. That sounded good.

He peered over the shrubs again. Bu-bu waved at him. She was standing at the far edge of the clearing. She pointed to something in the tall grass.

Annie was fast asleep in the grass!

Jack didn't know what to do. If he called her name, the gorillas would wake up. He had only one choice. He had to sneak over to her.

Jack put his book in his pack. He pushed past the shrubs and stepped into the clearing. His heart was pounding. He thought of the words from the book—*shy and gentle giants*.

As he started toward Annie, he heard a grunt. The giant gorilla with silver fur opened his eyes. When the gorilla saw Jack, he sat up.

Jack stopped in his tracks.

The gorilla just glared. *This* giant did not seem shy or gentle at all.

Jack saw a stick lying on the ground. He picked it up—just in case.

Jack's stick made the gorilla growl. He stood up. He was *very* tall and *very* wide.

Jack dropped his stick.

Bu-bu ran and hid behind a tree.

31

The silverback growled again. His long, shaggy arms touched the ground. His fingers curled under. Walking on his knuckles, he stepped toward Jack.

Jack stepped back.

The gorilla stepped forward.

Jack stepped back again.

The gorilla kept stepping forward. Jack kept stepping back until he had stepped out of the clearing.

But the silverback kept coming. Jack stumbled back through the brush until he came to a thick wall of plants.

The gorilla kept coming. Jack couldn't move back anymore.

"Uh . . . hi," he said nervously. He held up his hand. "I come in—"

Before Jack could say "peace," the giant gorilla went crazy. He hooted and leaped to his feet.

Jack crouched down in a panic.

The gorilla kept hooting. He grabbed a tree limb. He shook it wildly. He ripped leaves from branches.

He gnashed his teeth. He cupped his hands. He beat his chest.

WRAAGH! he roared. *WRAAGH!*

The gorilla dropped on all fours. He charged back and forth past Jack. Then he threw himself on his belly. He began bashing the ground with his palms. He bashed and bashed and bashed.

Jack scrambled on his hands and knees over to a tree. He hid behind the trunk, hugging his head.

He waited for the maniac gorilla to find him and tear him to pieces.

6

Good Morning, Gorillas

The pounding ended. There was silence . . . a long silence.

Jack opened his eyes. He peeked around the tree. The silverback was sitting on the ground. His lips were curved in a smile. He looked pleased with himself.

Was his whole act a fake? Jack wondered.

Jack didn't know whether to be scared or to laugh. The only thing he *did* know was he still had to get to Annie!

Jack pulled out the research book. He found the gorilla chapter again. He read:

> To safely get close to gorillas in the wild, it's wise to act like a gorilla yourself. Crouch down and rest on your knuckles like a gorilla. Keep your head down and act friendly!

Jack packed up his research book. He put his pack on his back. Then he went down on his knees.

Jack took a deep breath. He smiled a friendly smile. Pressing down on his knuckles, he moved out from behind the tree. His fingers hurt as he walked on them.

The silverback grunted.

Jack didn't look up. He kept smiling a friendly smile as he crawled through the brush toward the clearing.

When he got to the edge of the clearing, he glanced back. The giant gorilla was following him. He was frowning, but he didn't seem about to attack.

Jack kept going. He moved into the clearing. Then he stopped.

More gorillas were waking up. A large gorilla hugged Bu-bu as if to comfort her.

When Bu-bu saw Jack, she screeched joyfully.

All the other gorillas turned to look at him. They made nervous sounds.

Jack's heart pounded. But he just smiled his friendly smile and kept crawling. He crawled around the gorillas and over to Annie.

"Wake up!" he said, shaking her.

Annie yawned, then opened her eyes.

"Oh, hi!" she said.

"Are you okay?" asked Jack.

"Sure," she said. She sat up and looked around. She gasped.

The gorillas were staring at Jack and Annie with bright, darting eyes. The silverback stared the hardest.

"Oh, wow!" said Annie. A joyful smile crossed her face. "Good morning, gorillas!"

7

Eating Out

Annie kept smiling at the gorillas. "Wow!" she said. "Wow, wow, wow."

"Didn't you know you were sleeping next to them?" Jack asked.

"No!" she said. "When you didn't come back, Bu-bu led me here. But I couldn't see anything. It was too dark."

Just then, Bu-bu left her mother's arms and bounded over to Annie. She climbed into Annie's lap and hugged her.

Another small gorilla left his mother and ran over to Annie, too. He was about the size of a two-year-old kid.

"*Ho, ho!*" he said. He gave Annie a playful poke.

"Ho, ho yourself!" said Annie. "Is Ho-ho your name?"

She tickled Ho-ho. She tickled Bu-bu, too. The two small gorillas made laughing sounds and fell onto their backs.

The two mother gorillas laughed, too. *Huh-huh-huh*, they said.

Jack felt a little jealous. He wanted the gorillas to like him as well. But he didn't know how to join in the fun. So he just sighed and pulled out his notebook. He added to his "gorilla behavior" list:

gorillas like to tickle and laugh

41

Suddenly, he heard a low growl.

He looked up. The silverback had moved closer to him. He was glaring.

"That big guy doesn't understand what you're doing!" Annie called to Jack. "He's never seen anyone take notes before."

Jack quickly put his notebook away.

The giant gorilla huffed. Then he turned to his family and gave a short bark.

The gorillas began lining up behind the silverback. The baby traveled in his mother's arms. Ho-ho traveled on his mother's back. Bu-bu and Annie held hands. They all followed the silverback out of the clearing.

"Come on!" Annie called to Jack. "Let's go with Big Guy and the gang!"

Jack shook his head.

"I don't think they want *me* to come along," he said.

Bu-bu screeched at Jack. She held out her free hand to him.

"*Bu-bu* wants you!" said Annie.

Jack smiled shyly. He took Bu-bu's small, warm hand. Then he walked with Annie and the gorillas out of the clearing.

On their ramble through the cloud forest, the gorillas found food everywhere. They munched flowers and ferns and leaves. They swallowed and burped.

They munched twigs and branches and pieces of bark and bamboo. They swallowed and burped.

As the gorillas ate breakfast, it started to rain again. But they didn't seem to mind.

Annie didn't seem to mind, either. She and Bu-bu played tag in the drizzly woods. They ran around the trees, laughing and screeching.

Jack tried to follow them, but he gave up. He was tired and cold. Shivering, he stood under a mossy tree to keep dry.

While he was alone, Jack sneaked his notebook out of his pack. He made a new list:

<u>gorilla foods</u>

flowers

ferns

leaves

twigs

bark

branches

bamboo

As he wrote, he heard a low growl. He looked up.

Big Guy had spotted him. The silverback

was standing close by. He was frowning at Jack, his lips tucked in a tight line.

"Sorry, sorry!" said Jack. He quickly put away his notebook.

Big Guy kept frowning.

Jack quickly tried to act like a gorilla. He went down on all fours. He tore off the leaf of a plant. He took a bite. It tasted bitter, like vinegar. Jack pretended to munch and swallow and burp.

Big Guy huffed, then moved on. As soon as he was gone, Jack spat out the leaf.

"Yuck, yuck, yuck!" he said, wiping his tongue.

Jack felt a tap on his back. He jumped. But it was just Ho-ho. The small gorilla offered him a twig to eat.

"Oh, no thanks, Ho-ho," said Jack.

Ho-ho kept holding out the twig.

"Oh, okay," said Jack, politely taking it. "I'll eat it later." He put the twig into his backpack.

Ho-ho's mom came over to Jack. She held some berries to his lips.

"Uh, no thanks," Jack said.

The gorilla stared at him with a sad look.

"Oh, okay," said Jack. He opened his mouth. And Ho-ho's mom fed him the berries.

Jack munched the berries. To his surprise, they tasted good. He swallowed, then burped just like a gorilla. This time, he wasn't pretending.

Bu-bu's mom then came over to Jack. She offered him some rainwater from a cupped plant. Jack was very thirsty. He sipped the water. It tasted fresh and cold.

Bu-bu's mom took Jack's hand in her wide hand. She led him through the forest to Annie and Bu-bu.

Bu-bu screeched happily when she saw Jack. She threw her furry arms around him.

"Hi! We missed you!" Annie said to Jack. "Are you having fun?"

Jack smiled and nodded.

Actually, he *was* having fun now. He didn't mind the rain so much anymore. He didn't feel so left out. Some of the gorillas really seemed to like him, he thought. They seemed to like him a lot.

8

A Special Language

The rain ended. Slowly the feeding came to a stop.

Big Guy led his family into a clearing. The tall grass sparkled with misty sunlight.

The silverback lay down and tucked his arms under his head.

The other gorillas gathered around him. Some beat the grasses until they were flat.

Ho-ho's mom made a bed of weed stalks for Ho-ho. Bu-bu's mom made a bed of leaves for Bu-bu. Then she made two extra beds for Jack and Annie.

They lay down with all the gorillas to take their naps. Jack used his backpack for a pillow.

Lying on his leafy bed, Jack watched the mother of the baby gorilla groom her small baby. The mother parted his hair and searched through it, picking at his skin now and then.

The baby soon wiggled free and crawled around in the grass. His mother's gaze then rested on Annie. She moved over to Annie and gently grabbed one of her pigtails. She studied it carefully.

"What are you doing?" Annie asked.

"She's looking for bugs, I think," said Jack.

"Oh, yuck!" said Annie, sitting up.

Jack laughed. Just then, the baby's mother reached for him.

"Oops! No thanks! No bugs on me!" he said, and he sat up, too.

The mother gorilla lay back in the grass and closed her eyes. Her baby crawled over to Annie.

"Hi, Little Guy," Annie said tenderly. She picked up the baby and stroked his head. The baby smiled at her and closed his eyes.

While all the gorillas napped, Jack sneaked the book out of his pack. He found the gorilla chapter. He read softly to Annie:

> **Gorillas are very smart. A captive gorilla named Koko has even learned sign language. Sign language is a special language used by people who cannot hear. Koko can say—**

"*What?*" Annie said loudly. "*Sign* language? A *special language*?"

Her voice woke Bu-bu and Ho-ho. They sat up and rubbed their eyes.

"So?" said Jack.

"Morgan's secret *rhyme!*" said Annie. "Don't you remember?" She repeated the rhyme:

> *To find a special kind of magic*
> *in worlds so far apart,*
> *speak a special language,*
> *talk with your hands and heart.*

"Oh . . . yeah!" said Jack.

"I even know a little sign language," said Annie. "In school, we learned how to sign *I love you.*"

Annie held up a closed hand. Slowly she lifted her thumb, index finger, and little finger. She showed the sign to Bu-bu and Ho-ho.

"I—love—you," she said slowly.

The small gorillas looked curious.

Jack made the sign, too.

"I—love—you," he said to Bu-bu and Ho-ho.

The two little gorillas stared at Annie and Jack. Then both of them held up their hands. They tried to make the same sign.

"They love us, too!" said Annie.

"Wow," said Jack. He glanced over at Big Guy.

The silverback's eyes were open! He was watching them. Jack quickly closed the book. To his relief, the giant gorilla turned over.

"Well," Annie said with a sigh, "I guess that does it."

"We spoke a special language," said Jack. "We talked with our—" Before he could finish his sentence, Bu-bu pushed him.

"Whoa!" said Jack.

Ho-ho held his little arms above his head. He reared back and charged at Jack. With a flying tackle, he knocked Jack over.

"What's going on?" said Jack.

"They want to play with you!" said Annie.

Bu-bu jumped on Jack and put him in a headlock. Jack broke free from the two small gorillas. He jumped up and dashed into the forest.

Bu-bu and Ho-ho charged after him.

Annie carried Little Guy and followed. She laughed as the small gorillas looked for Jack.

Jack hid behind a tree. He pushed his glasses into place. He waited for Bu-bu.

In a moment, she walked by.

"BOO!" Jack shouted, jumping out.

Bu-bu screeched and leaped straight up in the air. Jack cracked up laughing.

Bu-bu didn't laugh, though. She bit her lip. She hid her face behind her hands.

"Ohhh, Bu-bu," said Annie. "Don't be scared."

She gently put the baby on the ground. She reached out to comfort Bu-bu.

Bu-bu wrapped her arms around Annie's

neck. She buried her furry head in Annie's shoulder.

"Jack was just playing," said Annie.

Bu-bu raised her head. She looked at Jack over Annie's shoulder.

"Friends?" he asked softly.

Bu-bu stuck her tongue out at him.

Jack laughed. Bu-bu showed her teeth in a big smile.

"Friends!" said Jack.

Just then, Ho-ho started screeching. Jack and Annie looked around. Ho-ho was pointing into the bushes.

"Where's Little Guy?" said Annie. She and Jack dashed around the shrubs.

The baby had crawled to a tree. He was looking up at a branch.

A huge, sleek cat with black fur was sitting on the branch. His pale green eyes stared down at the baby gorilla. He looked hungry.

"*A black leopard,*" breathed Jack.

The leopard leaped lightly down from his perch. He faced Little Guy. The baby looked scared.

"No!" cried Annie.

She ran over to the baby gorilla and scooped him into her arms.

The leopard let out a snarl. He lowered his head and started slowly toward Annie and the baby.

Jack panicked. He didn't know what to do at first. Then he remembered Big Guy's act. Jack took a deep breath. When he let it out, he made a loud hooting sound.

He tore out from the brush. Hooting like a silverback, he ran between Annie and the leopard.

Jack grabbed a tree limb and shook it. He ripped leaves from branches.

He cupped his hands. He beat his chest.

"WRAAGH!" he roared. *"WRAAGH!"*

Then Jack leaned over and charged back and forth past the leopard.

Finally, he threw himself on his belly. He began bashing the ground with his palms. He bashed and bashed and bashed.

"Jack!" Annie called. "Jack!"

Jack looked up.

"He's gone," Annie said in a quiet voice. "The leopard's gone. He left a while ago."

"Oh," said Jack.

He sat up.

He pushed his glasses into place. He looked around. Then he smiled.

9

Good-bye, Gorillas

Jack couldn't stop smiling. He had scared off a leopard!

Bu-bu and Ho-ho stared at Jack with awe. Annie looked at him with awe, too.

"When did you learn to do *that*?" she asked.

Before Jack could answer, he heard a rustling in the brush. Then Big Guy stepped out from the shrubs.

The giant gorilla walked silently over to Annie. He took Little Guy from her and put the baby on his back. Then he touched Annie's cheek gently.

Annie grinned at him.

Bu-bu and Ho-ho ran to Big Guy and clung to his legs.

The giant gorilla barked at the small ones, directing them to come with him.

As he walked past Jack, Big Guy stopped.

Huh-huh-huh, he said in a low voice. He reached out toward Jack.

Jack ducked.

But the silverback patted him on the head. Then he and the small gorillas moved out of sight.

Jack felt as if the top of his head were glowing.

"Wow," he whispered. "Did you see what he just did?"

"Yeah," said Annie. "He must have

watched the show you put on. He was proud of you."

"Well, he was proud of you, too," Jack said modestly.

Annie nodded, smiling. "I guess it's time to leave now," she said.

"Leave?" said Jack.

"We have to say good-bye now," said Annie.

"Good-bye?" said Jack. He didn't want to say good-bye to the gorillas. He loved them. They were totally great.

"Yeah," Annie said softly. "Come on."

She led the way back through the shrubs, around the trees, to the clearing.

They found all the gorillas awake. Some were stretching and yawning. Others were munching on grass or leaves.

The baby was back in his mother's arms. Bu-bu and Ho-ho were chattering away to their moms.

They're probably telling them what I did, Jack thought.

He and Annie walked over to Big Guy and stood in front of him. The other gorillas gathered around.

"We have to go now," Annie said to all of them.

"We have to say good-bye," said Jack.

"Thanks for letting us be a part of your family," said Annie.

She and Jack held up their hands and waved. The gorillas looked sad. They murmured soft sounds.

Big Guy lifted his hand in the air as if he were about to wave. But instead, the silverback raised his thumb, his index finger, and his little finger.

I love you, the giant gorilla signed.

Jack couldn't believe his eyes.

Annie signed back, *I love you*.

Jack signed, too.

The silverback stared at them for a long moment with a gentle, shy look. Then he turned away and gave a short bark to his family.

All the gorillas lined up behind him. The baby's mother held her baby close. Ho-ho rode piggyback on his mom. Bu-bu held her mom's hand.

The silverback started away from the clearing. The others followed.

Bu-bu was the only one who looked back. She screeched and waved at Jack and Annie. Then she walked away, out of sight.

Jack couldn't talk. His heart was too full. He took a few steps in the direction of the gorillas.

"Hey—" Annie said softly. "You're going the wrong way."

Jack looked back at her.

"The tree house is over there," she said. She pointed in the opposite direction—at the tree house peeking out from the fog.

Jack sighed. Then he turned and started to follow her out of the clearing.

"Oh, don't forget this," said Annie.

She leaned over and picked up Jack's backpack from the grass. She handed it to him.

"Thanks," he said.

They kept walking.

"And don't forget *this*," said Annie. She picked up Jack's jacket from under a tree. She handed it to him.

"Thanks," said Jack. He tied his jacket around his waist. They kept walking.

"And don't forget *these*," said Annie. She pointed to the flashlight and umbrella. They lay on the grass under the wide, mossy limbs of a fat tree.

Annie picked them up and carried them herself.

It started to drizzle again just as she and Jack got to the rope ladder. They climbed up into the tree house.

When they got inside, they looked out the window. Jack hoped to catch one last glimpse of the gorilla family.

But there was nothing to see. A white mist covered the cloud forest.

Annie picked up the Pennsylvania book. She pointed to a picture of Frog Creek woods.

"I wish we could go home," she said.

Suddenly, a joyous screech rang out. The

happy, wild sound shot through the white mist, through the cool rain, straight into Jack's heart.

He opened his mouth to answer the call of the gorillas. But it was too late. The wind began to blow.

The tree house started to spin.

It spun faster and faster.

Then everything was still.

Absolutely still.

10

A Special Magic

Tap-tap-tap.

Jack opened his eyes.

The Frog Creek woods were still dark and rainy.

"We're home," Annie said.

Jack sighed.

"I miss them already," he said.

"Me too," said Annie. "Did you take a lot of notes on their habits and behavior?"

Jack shrugged.

"I listed a few things about them," he said. "But sometimes lists don't tell you much. You have to love gorillas to *really* know them."

"Yeah. That's right," said Annie.

Jack opened his backpack. He pulled out their research book and put it in the corner.

Then he pulled out the twig that Ho-ho had given him. He smiled as he showed it to Annie.

"I promised Ho-ho I'd eat this later," he said. "But I think we should save it for Morgan instead."

"Good idea," said Annie. "It'll prove to her that we found a special magic."

"Yeah, *gorilla* magic," said Jack.

"The magic of *all* animals," said Annie.

"Yeah," said Jack.

He placed the twig next to the scrolls they'd brought back from old England.

"Let's go," said Annie. She started down.

Jack pulled on his backpack. He put the flashlight in his pack. Then he grabbed the umbrella and followed Annie.

They started through the Frog Creek woods. It was still cool and dark and rainy.

Jack didn't mind, though. He didn't put on his jacket. He didn't take out the flashlight. He didn't put up the umbrella.

Jack felt as if he weren't completely human yet. There was still a bit of gorilla left in him.

"*Ho, ho, ho,*" he said in a low voice.

"*Bu, bu,*" Annie said back.

"*Huh, huh, huh,*" they said together.

MORE FACTS FOR
JACK AND ANNIE AND *YOU*!

Gorillas are the biggest members of the group of animals we call *primates*. Other primates include chimpanzees, orangutans, gibbons, baboons, monkeys, and humans.

All gorillas live in Africa. There are three groups of gorillas—western lowland gorillas, eastern lowland gorillas, and mountain gorillas. Mountain gorillas are the largest gorillas. They have longer hair and longer jaws and teeth than lowland gorillas.

Mountain gorillas live in the volcanic mountains of Virunga in east-central Africa. The word *virunga* means "a lonely mountain that reaches to the clouds."

Gorillas are mainly *herbivores*, or plant-eaters. They keep on the move, so they will not deplete a feeding area. A silverback gorilla can eat up to 50 pounds of forest vegetation in only one day.

ENDANGERED SPECIES

All gorillas are on the endangered species list. But the ones most threatened are the mountain gorillas. Fewer than 650 still live in the wild. None live in captivity. A woman named Dian Fossey lived for almost 20 years with the mountain gorillas. During her life, she fought very hard for their protection.

GORILLAS AND
AMERICAN SIGN LANGUAGE

Since 1971, a lowland gorilla named Koko has been part of a gorilla language project in California. Gorillas will never be able to talk like people because their vocal cords cannot make the necessary range of sounds. But a woman named Penny Patterson taught Koko the gorilla how to use *American Sign Language*. American Sign Language is a special language using hand gestures. It is primarily used by people who are unable to hear. Koko has learned to make more than 1,000 signs. And she understands about 2,000 English words. She proves that gorillas have extraordinary intelligence, as well as many thoughts and feelings similar to those of humans.

Discover the facts behind the fiction!

Do you love the *real* things you find
out in the Magic Tree House books?
Join Jack and Annie as they share all the
great research they've done about the
cool places they've been in the

MAGIC TREE HOUSE®
RESEARCH GUIDES

The must-have companions for your favorite
Magic Tree House adventures!

Don't miss the next Magic Tree House book,
when Jack and Annie meet the Pilgrims and
nearly burn dinner in . . .

MAGIC TREE HOUSE® #27

THANKSGIVING ON THURSDAY

September 2003

Where have *you* traveled in the

MAGIC TREE HOUSE®?

#1–4: The Mystery of the Tree House*

#5–8: The Mystery of the Magic Spell*

☐ **#5 NIGHT OF THE NINJAS** Jack and Annie go to old Japan and learn the secrets of the ninjas.

☐ **#6 AFTERNOON ON THE AMAZON** Jack and Annie go to the Amazon rain forest and are greeted by army ants, crocodiles, and flesh-eating piranhas.

☐ **#7 SUNSET OF THE SABERTOOTH** Jack and Annie go back to the Ice Age—the world of woolly mammoths, sabertooth tigers, and a mysterious sorcerer.

☐ **#8 MIDNIGHT ON THE MOON** Jack and Annie go *forward* in time and explore the moon.

#9–12: The Mystery of the Ancient Riddles*

☐ **#9 DOLPHINS AT DAYBREAK** Jack and Annie take a mini-submarine into the world of sharks and dolphins.

☐ **#15 VIKING SHIPS AT SUNRISE** Jack and Annie visit a monastery in medieval Ireland on the day the Vikings attack!

☐ **#16 HOUR OF THE OLYMPICS** Jack and Annie go back to ancient Greece and the first Olympic games.

#17–20: The Mystery of the Enchanted Dog*

☐ **#17 TONIGHT ON THE TITANIC** Jack and Annie travel back to the decks of the *Titanic* and help two children escape from the sinking ship.

☐ **#18 BUFFALO BEFORE BREAKFAST** Jack and Annie go back in time to the Great Plains, where they meet a Lakota boy and stop a buffalo stampede!

☐ **#19 TIGERS AT TWILIGHT** Jack and Annie are whisked to a forest in India, where they are stalked by a hungry tiger!

☐ **#20 DINGOES AT DINNERTIME** Jack and Annie go to Australia and help a baby kangaroo and a koala bear escape from a wildfire.

#21–24: The Mystery of Morgan's Library

#25–28: The Mystery of Morgan's Rhymes

❑ **#25 STAGE FRIGHT ON A SUMMER NIGHT** Jack and Annie travel to Elizabethan England and help William Shakespeare put on a play.

Are you a fan of the Magic Tree House series?

Visit our

Web site

at

www.randomhouse.com/magictreehouse

Exciting sneak previews of the new book.
Games, puzzles, and other fun activities.
Contests with super prizes.
And much more!

Join Jack and Annie as they go on a quest
to save Camelot in a special hardcover
Magic Tree House® book!

A STEPPING STONE BOOK™

Great authors write great books . . .
for fantastic first reading experiences!

Grades 1–3

Duz Shedd series
  by Marjorie Weinman Sharmat
Junie B. Jones series by Barbara Park
Magic Tree House® series
  by Mary Pope Osborne
Marvin Redpost series by Louis Sachar

Clyde Robert Bulla
The Chalk Box Kid
The Paint Brush Kid
White Bird

J.C. Greenburg
#1 Andrew Lost on the Dog
#2 Andrew Lost in the Bathroom

Jackie French Koller
Mole and Shrew Are Two
Mole and Shrew All Year Through
Mole and Shrew Have Jobs to Do
Mole and Shrew Find a Clue

Jerry Spinelli
Tooter Pepperday
Blue Ribbon Blues: A Tooter Tale

Grades 2–4

A to Z Mysteries® series by Ron Roy
The Katie Lynn Cookie Company series
  by G. E. Stanley

Adèle Geras
Little Swan

**Stephanie Spinner &
Jonathan Etra**
Aliens for Breakfast
Aliens for Lunch
Aliens for Dinner

Gloria Whelan
Next Spring an Oriole
Silver
Hannah
Night of the Full Moon
Shadow of the Wolf

NONFICTION
Magic Tree House® Research G
  by Will Osborne and
  Mary Pope Osborne

Grades 3–5

The Magic Elements Quartet
  by Mallory Loehr
#1: Water Wishes
#2: Earth Magic
#3: Wind Spell
#4: Fire Dreams

Spider Kane Mysteries
  by Mary Pope Osborne
#1: Spider Kane and the Mystery Under
  the May-Apple
#2: Spider Kane and the Mystery at
  Jumbo Nightcrawler's

NONFICTION
Thomas Conklin
The *Titanic* Sinks!

Elizabeth Cody Kimmel
Balto and the Great Race

Look for these other books
by Mary Pope Osborne!

Picture books:
Kate and the Beanstalk
The Brave Little Seamstress
Moonhorse
Rocking Horse Christmas

For middle-grade readers:
Adaline Falling Star
American Tall Tales
The Deadly Power of Medusa
Favorite Greek Myths
Favorite Medieval Tales
Favorite Norse Myths
The Life of Jesus in Masterpieces of Art
Mermaid Tales from Around the World
One World, Many Religions
*Spider Kane and the Mystery Under
the May-Apple (#1)*
*Spider Kane and the Mystery at
Jumbo Nightcrawler's (#2)*
Standing in the Light

For young adult readers:
Haunted Waters